DISNEY

Bambi
and the
Great Prince
of the forest

Adapted by Christopher Nicholas
Illustrated by the Disney Storybook Artists

A Random House PICTUREBACK® Book
Random House 🏠 New York

Copyright © 2005 Disney Enterprises, Inc. All rights reserved under International and Pan-American Copyright Conventions.
Published in the United States by Random House Children's Books, a division of Random House, Inc., New York, and simultaneously
in Canada by Random House of Canada Limited, Toronto, in conjunction with Disney Enterprises, Inc. PICTUREBACK, RANDOM HOUSE,
and the Random House colophon are registered trademarks of Random House, Inc.

ISBN: 0-7364-2369-9   Library of Congress Control Number: 2005926653

www.randomhouse.com/kids/disney

Printed in the United States of America   10 9 8 7 6 5 4 3 2   First Random House Edition 2005

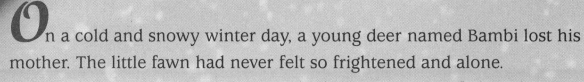

On a cold and snowy winter day, a young deer named Bambi lost his mother. The little fawn had never felt so frightened and alone.

A big, strong deer slowly approached. It was Bambi's father, the Great Prince of the Forest, who watched over all the woodland animals.

"Your mother can't be with you anymore," the Prince said gently. "Come, my son."

The Great Prince took Bambi back to his den, where they spent the night.

"Poor little fella, so young to be without his mother," Friend Owl said.

"I could use your help in finding a suitable doe to raise Bambi," the Great Prince told his feathered friend.

"Whooo better to raise the young prince . . . than the Great Prince himself!" Friend Owl suggested.

The Great Prince agreed to look after Bambi—but only until spring arrived. The Prince knew it would be difficult to watch over the whole forest and his son, too.

"Why don't you go with your friends to see the groundhog?" the Prince suggested one day.

"But I wanna stay with you," Bambi whined.

"I'll meet you later," the Prince responded, and turned to leave.

All the animals of the forest had gathered to watch the groundhog come out of his hole. Bambi met his friends there—Thumper the rabbit, Flower the skunk, and a beautiful young doe named Faline.

Just then, the groundhog appeared from his hole. The animals held their breath and waited. . . .

"No shadow!" the groundhog shouted gleefully.

All the animals were overjoyed that spring was coming!

Suddenly, a mean young deer named Ronno leaped out and shouted, "Boo!"

"Aaaahhh!" the groundhog screamed, and dove back into his hole.

Then Ronno started to tease Bambi. "Isn't that a girl's name?" he asked, trying to goad Bambi into a fight.

"Clobber him, Bambi!" Thumper shouted.

Luckily for Bambi, Ronno's mother called and he had to run off.

"See ya, Bambi," Thumper and Flower said as they left with their parents.

"Do you want us to walk you home?" Faline asked.

"No . . . my father's coming for me," Bambi said.

So Faline left with her family, and poor Bambi was all alone.

After a while, Bambi started to get sleepy, and he lay down for a nap. He was soon woken by the sound of . . . his mother's voice?

"Mother?" Bambi cried as he ran toward the sound. But it wasn't his mother—it was a hunter's deer call!

Bambi froze with fear as hunting dogs lunged toward him.

Fortunately, the Great Prince leaped out of the forest and fought the dogs off.

"Never freeze like that. Ever!" the Prince scolded as they raced off to safety.

"I'm . . . I'm sorry," Bambi said, sad that he had disappointed his father.

"I guess I'm not what a prince's son is supposed to be," Bambi told Thumper and Flower later that day. "If I could just show my dad that I can be brave, like him . . ."

"Being brave is easy! I can teach you," Thumper said, making his best brave face. "The trick is to be scarier than whatever is scaring you."

After a few lessons from Thumper, Bambi tried being brave with a porcupine. It didn't go very well. The young deer ended up with a back full of quills!

"How's it look?" Bambi asked.

"It ain't pretty," the rabbit responded.

Just as Thumper was pulling out the last porcupine quill, Ronno showed up. The mean young deer decided that this was a great time to tease Bambi about freezing in front of the hunters.

"If we didn't have cowards, we couldn't tell who the brave ones are," Ronno said smugly.

"I'm not a coward!" Bambi shouted. Then Thumper pushed him right into Ronno, who fell into the mud.

Furious, Ronno chased the two friends toward a cliff—and Bambi jumped across it with Thumper on his back! Ronno stopped in his tracks.

The Great Prince saw everything. "I didn't make a jump like that until I had antlers," he told his son.

Bambi felt so proud!

The next day, before heading out on his patrol, the Great Prince
turned to his son.

"The forest is waiting—are you coming?" the Prince asked.

Bambi couldn't have been more thrilled!

As days passed, Bambi and his father spent more and more time together and slowly got to know each other. Bambi even convinced the Prince to stop and play once in a while!

Weeks passed. The weather grew warmer, and winter slowly turned to spring. One day, as Bambi and the Prince were playing together, Friend Owl flew down.

"There you two are," the bird said. "There's someone I'd like you to meet."

Friend Owl introduced Mena—the doe he had found to take care of Bambi.

"You're sending me away?" Bambi asked.

"Bambi, a prince does not—" the Great Prince began.

"That's all you care about. Not about me!" Bambi cried. He ran off, heartbroken.

That afternoon, Bambi said goodbye to all his friends. Then he began to follow Mena to his new home in a different part of the forest. On the way, Mena accidentally fell into a deer trap.

Suddenly, a pack of snarling hunting dogs approached.

"Run, Bambi!" Mena shouted.

Bambi called out to the dogs, leading them away from Mena.

With the hungry dogs on his tail, Bambi dashed up a cliff—
and escaped the dogs! But the ground gave way, and the little
deer tumbled down.

Just then, the Great Prince arrived and raced to the fallen
deer's side. "Bambi!" he cried.

"Dad?" Bambi replied weakly.

The Prince was so happy that his son was all right. At that
moment, he realized that he couldn't stand the thought of losing
Bambi again. . . .

Days later, the Great Prince led Bambi to a part of the forest that he had never seen before.

"This is where I met your mother," the Prince said, opening up to his son for the first time. "I was just about your age."

"What were you like?" Bambi asked.

"I was a lot like you."